Three Boys and a Circus

Enid Blyton

Illustrations by Grace Lodge

WERNER LAURIE

Originally written under the
pen-name of "Mary Pollock"

Re-issued 1949

Printed by Odhams (Watford) Limited, of Watford, Herts,
for T. Werner Laurie, 187 Piccadilly, London, W.1

Contents

CHAPTER ONE

THE COMING OF THE CIRCUS

DICK sat under a hedge, eating his dinner. By him sat his dog, Bouncer, a shaggy-haired sheep-dog, his hair over his eyes. Bouncer was waiting for his share of the dinner.

It wasn't much of a dinner—two slices of very dry bread and a crumbly bit of cheese! But Dick thought he was lucky to have it. He had found it on the road-way, thrown away by a workman who didn't want it.

"Here you are, Bouncer—here's your share," said Dick, giving the dog half a piece of bread and a few crumbs of cheese. Bouncer gobbled them up in a trice and wagged his tail. He licked his master and whined.

"Oh, you want a drink, do you?" said Dick. "Well,

so do I. You must wait till we come to a farm, and we'll ask for some water."

"Woof!" said Bouncer—and then he pricked up his ears. He could hear strange sounds. Dick heard them, too.

"What's that?" he wondered, and he got up to see. The lane turned a corner not far off, and round the bend, over the tops of the hedges, could be seen bright-coloured vans and carts. There was the sound of music, too, and of gay voices calling to one another.

"It's a fair or a circus," said Dick. "We'll watch it pass by us, Bouncer. We don't often have a treat like this. Look—here they come. It's a circus!"

So it was. The whole circus was on the move, going to the next town to give a show. The long procession of vans and cages and carts moved slowly by Dick and Bouncer.

Some beautiful horses came first, trotting proudly along in a line. Two men were with them, one on the first horse and one on the last. Behind them came a clown, playing a merry tune on a big concertina. The clown was in his circus suit and his face was painted red and white. Dick laughed to see him for he danced about and round and round as he played, singing a funny song.

Everyone joined in the chorus. Some of the circus folk walked, others rode, and the rest drove their vans. There were a great many gay caravans, with bright curtains flapping in the wind, and smoke coming from tin chimneys on the roof. Dick thought they looked fine. There were cages, too, all with their sides shut, so that the animals inside should not be disturbed by the move.

"Woof!" barked Bouncer

"Hie! Look at the elephants!" yelled Dick in excitement. Two enormous grey beasts came plodding heavily into the lane, their backs piled with poles and boards, and their trunks swinging from side to side.

"Woof!" barked Bouncer, who did not like the smell of the elephants at all. Dick put a hand on his collar—and then he grinned for joy.

"The circus is going to have a rest here!" he said. "What luck! Now we can really see everything properly, Bouncer!"

The circus stopped. The horses were led away to a grassy field nearby. The vans pulled up in a line on one side of the lane. Six white goats that also belonged to the circus went to graze on the common behind Dick. The elephants knelt down for a rest.

Dick and Bouncer went to look at everything. They stopped in amazement at the sight of a small woman with five monkeys around her. She was talking to them as if they were children, and was laying a box for dinner.

"And just you see you don't have more than your fair share of bananas today!" she said to a small brighteyed monkey in a blue coat. Each monkey wore a different coloured coat, and a frilly collar. When they saw Bouncer they all leapt to the top of their caravan and sat there chattering.

"Go away, boy," said the monkey woman crossly. "Your dog has frightened my monkeys."

"Oh, can't I stay and watch them having their dinner?" begged Dick.

One of the monkeys took a flying leap and landed on Dick's shoulder. It took hold of his ear and pinched it gently. Dick was too surprised to move.

"Look at that!" said the monkey woman with a laugh. "All right—stand still. He won't hurt you. Let me take him."

Dick heard Bouncer barking at something, and when the monkey had been safely lifted from his shoulder, he hurried off to see what the noise was about.

Bouncer had found the elephants! He was telling them exactly what he thought about them, and he was being very rude! The elephants took no notice at all. Dick went to pick Bouncer up—and he felt a hand in his pocket! Somebody was feeling to see if he had anything there!

"Hie, stop that!" cried Dick, and clapped his hand to his pocket.

"Hrrrrumph!" said an elephant, and took the end of his trunk out of Dick's pocket. He held a piece of paper in it, and put it into his big mouth.

"Oh, so it was you, was it?" said Dick, surprised. "Well, you won't find that paper tastes very nice!"

"Now then, what are you doing here?" cried a loud voice, and a man dressed in riding-breeches and a bright yellow jersey came round a caravan. "Run away! We don't want a stranger upsetting our animals."

It was the owner of the circus, Mr. Monty Ravelini, a fine handsome man with black curly hair, bright black eyes, and ruddy cheeks.

"All right, sir," said Dick. He went round the line of caravans till he came to the last one. This was a fine big one, painted yellow and blue. It had blue curtains at the windows, and a bright yellow door at the back. Dick wondered who it belonged to. He thought he really must peep inside. He had never been into a caravan and had always wondered what they were like.

He stood on a wheel and hoisted himself up. Bouncer stood anxiously waiting. Dick parted the curtains and looked inside.

There was somebody there. A boy lay on a bunk-bed, his face turned to the wall. He was muttering hard to himself.

"It's too bad! It's too bad! I won't stand it—I won't, I won't!"

Dick's foot slipped on the wheel, and he made a noise. The boy turned round in the bunk at once and stared at Dick.

"Who are you, and what are you peeping in at me for?" he demanded angrily.

"I didn't know there was anyone here," said Dick. "I just wanted to see what the inside of a caravan was like."

"Grrrrrr!" said Bouncer from below the caravan. The boy in the bunk sat up.

"That's only my dog," explained Dick.

"Have you got a dog?" said the boy. "Well, I'd like to see him. Open the door and bring him in. What's he like?"

"He's an old English sheep-dog," said Dick. "Wait a minute and I'll bring him in!"

CHAPTER TWO

DICK MAKES FRIENDS WITH PEDRO

DICK jumped down from the window, picked up Bouncer, opened the door of the caravan and went inside. He looked round.

"What a lovely place!" he said. "Much better than living in a house, isn't it? It's got everything in it that anyone could want—tables, chairs, bunks, a stove, cupboards—everything! I wish *I* lived in a caravan like this."

"What's your dog's name?" asked the boy in the bunk. "Isn't he a fine dog! Come here, good fellow!"

"Look out!" said Dick warningly. "He won't let anybody pet him but me."

The boy in the bunk laughed. He pulled Bouncer on to his bed, and patted him with strong, kind hands. Bouncer whined with delight and licked the boy's face.

"Well, I've never seen Bouncer do that before to anyone but me," said Dick, rather jealous.

"I know all about dogs," said the boy. "I've got eight!"

"Eight! Good gracious! where are they?" asked Dick.

The boy pushed Bouncer away, lay down again and looked miserable.

"Somebody else is looking after them," he said. "I've hurt my legs and I can't see to them. But the awful part is I know the dogs hate the boy who's looking after them. Look here—I'll tell you all about it if you like!"

"Go on then," said Dick, and he sat down, with Bouncer beside him.

"My uncle is Mr. Ravelini, who owns this circus," said the boy. "I'm Pedro Ravelini, and this is my uncle's caravan. Well, I'm in charge of the dogs, and you should see the way they learn for me! I've got one dog that gets in a wooden train I made, and drives it round the ring by himself!"

"Have you really?" said Dick, astonished. "Do you go into the ring, then?"

"Of course," said Pedro. "I'm a circus boy. That's why your dog loved me when he saw me—he smells that I love dogs and animals of all kinds. I love horses, too—and that's how I hurt my legs."

"What happened?" asked Dick.

"Well, my uncle bought a fine new black horse," said Pedro. "He forbade me to ride it—but I did, and the horse threw me off and rolled on my legs. They do that sometimes, you know. Now I've got to stay here till my legs are better, and Uncle has put Larry in charge of my precious dogs, and I know they hate him!"

Pedro banged the bed clothes as if he were hitting Larry. Dick laughed. Bouncer jumped up on the bed and licked Pedro's chin over and over again.

"You're a nice fellow," said Pedro, hugging Bouncer. "You're a clever dog, too, I can see. I wish you were mine. How did you get him?"

"He's been mine ever since I found him in the road, hurt by a car," said Dick. "I ran away because of him!"

"Ran away! What do you mean?" said Pedro, puzzled. "Haven't you got a home, then?"

"No," said Dick. "I haven't a father or mother, and I was sent to a Home for Poor Children. When I found Bouncer hurt in the road, I smuggled him into a shed belonging to the Home, and looked after him; but when the Head found out, he was angry, and said Bouncer must go to a Dogs' Home. So I ran away with him."

"Did you really?" said Pedro. "How long is it since you've run away?"

"About three weeks," said Dick. "I'm always afraid somebody will find me and take me back to the Home again—without Bouncer. You see, Pedro, it's so lovely to have something to love, something that's your very own. That's why I wanted him so badly—and anyway, I always loved animals."

"I love animals, too," said Pedro. "All true circus people love them. We are kind to them, and—— Oh, listen—what's that?"

Such a noise of shouting and barking had broken out! Pedro sat up in his bunk, his face white.

"One of my dogs has bitten Larry," he groaned. "I knew that would happen. He isn't a real circus lad. He doesn't really belong to us. Oh, quick, Dick, go and see what's happening and come back and tell me!"

Dick sped out of the caravan with Bouncer. The two big elephants were standing up now, wondering what the excitement was about. The five monkeys were grouped together on the roof of their caravan, chattering in fright.

A half-grown lad was rubbing his leg and shouting angrily to a group of people around him. "Bit me on the angle, the brute! Just flew at me for nothing. Ah, but I gave him a good kick; serve him right! I won't look after the dogs any more."

"Go to Madame Sara and ask her to see to your leg," said Mr. Ravelini in a sharp voice. "Our dogs don't fly at people unless there is a good cause. In future you will help with the horses, Larry."

Larry limped off, his face red and angry, muttering all kinds of things to himself. Dick didn't like the look of him at all. He heard the sound of whimpering, and looked round. It came from a large cage nearby. The side was down, and a crowd of dogs ran excitedly to and fro in the cage. They were all smooth-haired fox terriers—bright-eyed little things, eager and sharp.

One little dog lay in a corner whimpering. "I expect that's the one that horrid Larry hit," said Dick, feeling angry. He went over to the cage. Nobody paid any attention to him—so quick as thought he slipped open the door, walked in, and went up to the little hurt dog.

"I'll take you to Pedro," said Dick, and he picked it up. Bouncer jumped up and sniffed. Then, trotting at Dick's heels, he went back to Pedro's caravan with him.

Dick told Pedro what had happened. Pedro was so angry that he tried to get out of his bunk, but he couldn't. His dog lay contentedly beside him.

"Get me that big pot of ointment, Dick," said Pedro, pointing to a large jar on a shelf. Dick got it, and together the two boys gently rubbed some of the ointment into the dog's skin.

"That awful Larry kicked you, didn't he?" said Pedro gently. "Well, he won't look after you any more. But who will? Everyone's so busy in the circus. Oh, bother my legs! Why did I try to ride that horse!"

Somebody looked into the caravan. It was Mr. Ravelini. When he saw Dick there, he frowned.

"Wasn't it you I told to go away not so long ago?" he asked angrily. "Go on—run off or I'll soon make you!"

"Oh, but Uncle——" began Pedro, seeing Dick's scared face—but the ringmaster roared at Pedro to be quiet.

"Am I master in my own circus or am I not?" he shouted. "If you had obeyed me, you would not have hurt yourself, and all this trouble today would not have happened!" He pushed Dick out of the caravan.

"Go, and don't come back!" he commanded. "Strangers upset our animals and make them restless. Take that dog with you!"

Dick picked up Bouncer and slipped down the caravan steps without even saying goodbye to Pedro. But he made up his mind to see him before the circus went on its way.

He hid behind a bush until he saw Mr. Ravelini leave the caravan and go to look at his beautiful horses. Then he shot up the steps of the caravan again and poked his head inside.

"Goodbye, Pedro!" he said. "Good luck!"

"Wait, wait!" called Pedro. "Come here—oh, wait a minute, Dick!"

Dick stood there, and Pedro spoke to him pleadingly.

"Dick! *Would* you just see if my dogs have fresh water in their cage?"

"Right!" said Dick. "Hope I don't get caught by your uncle, that's all!"

CHAPTER THREE

DICK GETS INTO TROUBLE—AND OUT OF IT!

DICK ran quietly to the dogs' big cage. All the circus folk were sitting having a kind of picnic meal on the common. No one was near. Dick looked into the dogs' cage.

There were two big water bowls—and both were empty! Two of the dogs stared at Dick, their tongues hanging out.

"You're thirsty!" said Dick. "I'll get you some water. You're thirsty, too, aren't you, Bouncer? Come on, we'll go to that stream over there."

Dick picked up a big pail and set off to the stream. Bouncer lapped thirstily at the water. Dick filled the pail and went back to the dogs. He slipped inside the cage and filled the bowls. All the dogs ran to drink. Dick looked round their cage.

"Filthy dirty!" he said. "I guess that horrid Larry hasn't cleaned their cage for ages. I've a good mind to do it!"

He ran back to Pedro and told him. "Would you really clean their cage for me?" asked the boy eagerly. "Well, I'll tell you where the scrubbing-brush, disinfectant, and everything is kept. But whilst you are doing it, Dick, you'd better bring all the dogs in here to me. You can't clean out their cage with them all round you. I say, you *are* a brick!"

"I'll go and get the dogs," said Dick, not thinking it at all a strange thing to do. He went off to the cage, and let out all the seven dogs. The eighth one was still with Pedro. "Come on, come on," said the boy, and he led them to the caravan.

They came after him willingly, sniffing at Bouncer, who was astonished but pleased to have so many playmates all of a sudden. Dick took them up the steps of the caravan. They rushed in at the door, yelping with joy to see Pedro.

The boy went quite mad with delight. He got all the dogs on to his bed and hugged them wildly. Dick saw that he had tears in his eyes, and he guessed how much Pedro loved his dogs.

"Oh, thank you, Dick," said the boy. "It's the first time I've seen them since I got my legs hurt."

"I'll go and get on with the cleaning," said Dick. He went off to the cage. He set to work with a will, and soon the cage was washed and scrubbed from end to end, and smelt of good disinfectant. Dick was quite proud of his work when he had finished.

Then Madame Sara, who owned the five monkeys, came up and stared at him in surprise. "What's this?" she asked. "Who told you to do that? And where are the dogs?"

"Oh, I let them out," said Dick, emptying the dirty water out of his pail, "You see, I——"

"Let them out!" squealed Madame Sara, in horror. "Let them out! Don't you know those are valuable dogs! Ravelini! Ravelini! This boy has let out your dogs!"

Ravelini came hurrying up, his face as black as thunder. Dick took one look at him and decided not to wait. He ran! How he ran! He didn't stop till he was right down the road and round the corner.

And then he discovered that he hadn't got Bouncer with him! Goodness! Now what was he to do? He couldn't *possibly* leave Bouncer behind. He sat under a hedge and thought hard. Where was Bouncer? Oh—of course—he was in Pedro's caravan, having a good time with all the other dogs. Well, he must get him back, that was quite certain.

Dick was tired. He had walked a long way that day and he had cleaned out a very large cage. He lay down, with the sun warming him, and shut his eyes. Before he knew it he was fast asleep.

When he woke up, the circus was gone. Dick stared at the place where it had rested for an hour or two, and his heart sank. What about Bouncer?

"Bouncer, Bouncer!" he called, and then he whistled loudly. But no Bouncer came. Dick stared round in dismay. He felt terribly lonely without his shaggy sheep-dog at his ankles. He must get him back somehow!

"I shall follow the circus," thought Dick. "Then when it settles into camp I'll go and find Pedro again and get back Bouncer."

So he set off to the next town, walking as fast as he could. A kind woman gave him some bread and jam for his tea.

On he went again, and towards night came to a big field outside the nearby town.

And there he heard the sound of the little clown's concertina playing once more.

"The circus is in that field!" thought Dick joyfully, and he crept up to the hedge. It was dark, but there were two or three camp fires glowing in the field, and the circus folk sat round them, tired after their long day. Two huge shapes stood under a great elm tree. Dick guessed they were the elephants. He wished that he belonged to the camp. It looked so friendly and so exciting as he stood there on the other side of the hedge.

Dick looked for Mr. Ravelini's caravan, where Pedro lay in bed. It was near a camp fire!

"I can't possibly go and speak to Pedro yet," thought Dick. "I should be seen—and I guess Mr. Ravelini would whip me well if he caught me round the circus again!"

Not far away was a small cart, in which were piled a great many wooden benches that were used in the circus ring. Dick squeezed through the hedge and made his way to it. He crept underneath, and lay there, waiting for the circus folk to go to their caravans. He had not yet made up his mind how to look for Bouncer.

As he lay there he saw some queer white shapes

moving round the cart. He could not imagine what they were—but when one of them began to nibble his shoe, he gave a yell that made all the circus folk prick up their ears.

A lantern flashed in his direction—and Dick saw that the queer white figures he had seen were only the six beautiful white circus goats! How he wished he hadn't yelled like that! He lay quiet, hoping that nobody would see him.

But Larry spotted him and dragged him out from underneath the cart. "Got you!" he cried. "Got you! What are you doing round our camp—come to steal something? You just come to Mr. Ravelini!"

"No, no!" yelled poor Dick. The last thing he wanted was to see Mr. Ravelini again. He struggled hard—but Larry held his arms in a tight grip, and jerked him over to Mr. Ravelini's camp fire.

"So!" said the ringmaster in surprise. "We meet again! What do you want now?"

"Only my dog Bouncer, please, sir," said Dick in a fright.

"Don't be afraid," said Ravelini in a gentle voice. "I know now what you were doing this morning—you were cleaning out that dirty cage for Pedro—and you had given him the dogs. I can tell you I was surprised when I opened my caravan door and saw all those dogs on Pedro's bed."

"Is Bouncer here, please?" asked Dick anxiously.

"He's with Pedro," said Ravelini. "Let this boy go, Larry. He did what you hadn't done and *should* have done, you lazy good-for-nothing fellow—gave the dogs water and cleaned their cage!"

Larry scowled, but did not dare to say anything to

the ringmaster. He let go Dick's arm, but pinched it hard before he dropped it.

"You can go and find Bouncer," said Mr. Ravelini. "He's in my caravan. And wait—are you hungry?"

"Yes, sir," said Dick.

Madame Sara ladled a large mug of soup from the big black pot on the fire.

"There you are," she said. "Pedro has some bread. Go and ask him for it."

Dick sped off to Pedro's caravan, being careful not to spill the fine-smelling soup. There was a light in the caravan. Dick knocked and opened the door.

"Gracious! It's you!" cried Pedro—and Bouncer leapt right off the bed, and nearly knocked the mug of soup out of Dick's hand. Dick put the soup down and hugged his yelping dog.

The two boys were very pleased to see each other again. They told one another all that had happened, whilst Dick ate his hot soup, and dipped big pieces of bread into it. Bouncer licked out the mug when Dick had finished. The little, hurt dog, Leppi, was still on Pedro's bed, and looked solemnly at the boys whilst they talked.

"Where are you going to sleep tonight?" said Pedro.

"In a haystack, if I can find one," said Dick. "It's a nice warm place, but a bit tickly. Bouncer makes a good hot-water bottle!"

"Stay here and sleep in our caravan," said Pedro. "Do you know what I'm going to do, Dick? I'm going to ask my uncle if he'll let you stay on with me till I'm well enough to look after our dogs again—and you can look after them till then! How would you like that?"

"Fine!" said Dick in surprise and delight. "Will he let me, do you think?"

"I'm sure he will," said Pedro. "He's got a good heart, though he shouts and roars. Look, pull out that old roll of mattress just there, and put it below my bunk. I'll give you one of my blankets. Bouncer will do for a pillow!"

Dick did as he was told. He unrolled the little mattress and lay down. Bouncer would not be a pillow, so Dick took a cushion from a chair. He rolled Pedro's blanket round him.

"First time I've slept in a caravan," he said. "It's fun. I like it! Good night, Pedro."

"Good night," said Pedro—and then both the boys fell asleep, each with a dog cuddled up to him. They did not wake when Mr. Ravelini came to bed himself. He held up the lamp and looked at the two sleeping boys, one on the floor and one in the bunk.

The two dogs woke and growled softly. The ringmaster chuckled. "Growl away!" he said. "Growl away! Well, well, it's a crowded caravan tonight—we'd better leave the door open for a little air!"

He left the door open and blew out the lamp. The cool summer night crept in, and the stars looked down. The camp slept peacefully. Only the six goats stirred now and again, white shadows underneath a caravan.

CHAPTER FOUR

MR. RAVELINI'S CIRCUS

It was fun to wake up in the morning and see the sun shining in through the open door of the caravan. Dick sat up and looked out. Bouncer sat up too, and yawned widely.

Leppi, the little dog on Pedro's bed, awoke at their movements and jumped down to Bouncer. That woke Pedro, and he sat up and grinned at Dick.

Soon there was a bustle in the blue and yellow caravan. Dick helped to set the breakfast on a small table. Mr. Ravelini looked in the cupboard and found a large packet of sausages. Soon they were frying in a pan over the stove, and a delicious smell filled the air.

"Uncle," said Pedro, as they all sat eating their

breakfasts, "somebody's got to look after the dogs if Larry doesn't. Could you let Dick do the job till I'm well again? He's good with dogs."

"So I saw," said Mr. Ravelini, putting half a sausage into his big mouth. He chewed it up and looked at Dick. Dick wished that he could be like Bouncer, and sit up and beg to Mr. Ravelini. But all he could do was to look at him pleadingly.

"All right," said the ringmaster, cutting up his fourth sausage. "All right. He can stay, Pedro—but mind you, he goes the first time anything goes wrong! I won't have another Larry here!"

"Oh, thank you, sir!" said Dick, almost choking with delight. "I'll do my best."

"Good!" said Pedro, jerking up and down in his bunk. "Oh, good!"

"Pedro!" said his uncle. "You are shaking the whole caravan! What will the doctor say? He comes today, and you know that he said you must keep as still as possible."

When Mr. Ravelini went out to look at his beloved horses, Dick brought water and towel to Pedro, and helped him to wash. He made his bunk again as best he could, and then washed up the breakfast things.

"You needn't bother to do all that," said Pedro. "Old Mother Dooly comes to do everything. Here she is!"

An old woman poked her head in at the door, and nodded to the two boys. "So we've got a new fellow, have we?" she said. "Well, you look a good strong boy. That Larry's a bad one—I missed a pair of kippers yesterday, and well do I know who took them!"

"I'll go and see to the dogs now," said Dick. "I'll be back later, Pedro." Off he went. The dogs were wild with delight to see him. He fed them, gave them fresh water, and then went to ask Mr. Ravelini if he could take them out for a run.

"Yes," said Ravelini, "but take Larry with you. You can't manage the lot. Not at first, anyway."

Dick didn't at all want Larry to go with him, but he dared not disobey. He went to tell him. Larry was rubbing down a big black horse, and he scowled at Dick.

"I'm coming," he said. "Think you're mighty clever, don't you, just walking into a job like this! But it won't last long—not if I can help it, anyhow!"

Dick took no notice. Larry was bigger than he was, and he didn't want a fight. Together they went to the dogs' cage. Larry took down the leads and harness. Each dog wore a kind of harness round its front legs and chest, so that his neck would not be pulled by a collar. Ravelini was very particular about his dogs, and liked them kept in perfect health and comfort.

Larry clipped four of the dogs together, on long leads. Dick took the other three. Then off they went. Larry talked a lot. He told Dick all about the circus folk, but he seemed to dislike most of them.

"There's Charlie the clown," he said, as they passed a caravan painted red. "He may be funny in the ring but he's mighty gloomy out of it—except when he plays his old concertina."

The clown was dressed in old grey trousers and a dirty blue sweater. He was sitting on his caravan steps reading his newspaper. Bouncer ran up to sniff at him. Charlie lowered his paper and saw Dick. At once he rolled down the steps, stood on his hands, turned three cart-wheels one after the other, and ended up by looking at Dick between his legs in a most peculiar manner. Dick screamed with laughter, and Bouncer looked at Charlie in fright.

"My dog's not used to people behaving like that!" said Dick. "He thinks you're quite mad."

They passed the elephants with their keeper, Mr. Roony. He was oiling their skins, and had to have a ladder to reach the top part of their backs.

"What are the elephants' names?" asked Dick.

"Chum and Pal," said Larry. "Look out! Chum will blow your cap off if he can!"

Sure enough a draught of air raised Dick's cap from his head! It was one of Chum's little tricks. He trumpeted at Dick as he went by. Bouncer growled. He could not get used to such enormous creatures. He went a little too near, and Chum put out his trunk, twisted it gently round the dog's shaggy body and lifted him up in the air!

How Bouncer barked! "Put him down, you rascal, put him down!" roared Mr. Roony. "Would you be eating dog for your dinner then? Ah, you scamp!"

Dick looked so alarmed that Mr. Roony roared with laughter at him. "Don't fret," he said. "He'll not be eating your dog yet, youngster! He'd rather have a bun any day!"

Bouncer was put gently down to the ground and at once ran off, making up his mind that he would never, never go near elephants again.

They passed Madame Sara and her five monkeys, who were being fitted for new coats. Madame Sara loved her monkeys best in all the world, and spent all her money buying silks and satins and wools to make them new clothes. She sewed beautifully, and boasted that her monkeys were the best-dressed in the world, which was quite true.

Bouncer went up to sniff at the monkeys. He was a most inquisitive dog! A small monkey made a chattering noise, leapt on to Bouncer's back, and jigged up and down there as if he were a horse. Bouncer got such a fright that he tore off round the field. This was just what the monkey wanted! She sat there on his back, going up and down like a proper little rider, whist everyone looked on and laughed.

Madame Sara called her monkey. "Wendy! Wendy! Oh, you naughty girl! Come here at once!"

Wendy leapt off Bouncer, and ran back to Madame Sara. She leapt to her shoulder and coiled round her neck like a fur.

"Wendy is going to be very clever," said Madame Sara. "I think I will teach her to ride one of Pedro's dogs, Larry. I could make her a beautiful little riding-dress. She would love to gallop round the ring on Leppi or Tinker."

"Come on," said Larry, taking no notice of Madame Sara. "We can't spend all the morning in the field!"

They went by the great tent that was being put up in the middle of the field ready for the next performance. Dick peeped inside. There were three people practising there, and what marvellous things they were doing!

"Who are they?" asked Dick, in wonder, watching the marvellous jumps and leaps that the two men and one girl were doing.

Dick did not see what Larry was doing

"Oh, they're Philippo, Yosif, and Bella," said Larry. "They are the acrobats. You should see them swinging in the roof, leaping from one trapeze to another. They never fall, never."

"But don't they have a net under them, when they are swinging about like that?" asked Dick.

"Yes—but that's only to please the people who come to watch!" said Larry. "Philippo would never have it there himself! He once climbed up to the very top of the big tent and stood on one foot on the top of the flag post there."

"Good gracious!" said Dick, wishing that Philippo would do it again. "I should never dare to do a thing like that."

"You couldn't if you tried," said Larry. "Circus folk are born, not made! All of us have been in the show since we were babies!"

Dick remembered that Pedro had said that Larry didn't really belong to the circus folk, but he didn't like to say so. They left the circus field behind, and went out on the hills. It was lovely there. Larks rose up around them and sang madly in the sky. The sun poured down, and the boys felt very hot.

"We'll let the dogs have a rest," said Larry, who badly wanted a rest himself. They sat down under a tree. The dogs lay down, too, their tongues out, panting and happy.

Dick lay down on his back and looked up into the deep green of the tree. He felt very happy. He belonged to the circus for a little while! Bouncer sat near him, and licked his nose now and again.

Dick did not see what Larry was doing. Larry was slipping one of Dick's leads undone! He was setting

Tinker free! Tinker gave a surprised yelp and ran off to go rabbiting. He was delighted. Larry lay down and grinned.

"Isn't it about time to turn back now?" said Dick at last. He sat up. "It must be getting on for twelve."

Then he stared in horror at his dogs. One was gone! "Larry," he said, "where's that dog with the black head?"

"Who? Tinker?" said Larry, pretending to be very surprised. "Goodness! He's gone! You *will* get into a row, Dick—that's Ravelini's best dog! You *are* careless."

"I'm not!" cried Dick, springing to his feet. "That dog was on his lead when I lay down—and the end of his lead is in my hand still! Did you slip him loose?"

"I'll fight you if you say things like that!" said Larry fiercely.

"Oh, don't be a donkey," said Dick, worried. "We must find the dog. This isn't time for fighting!"

Dick whistled and whistled. Tinker didn't come.

Larry grinned to himself. He knew quite well that once Tinker got his head down a rabbit hole, only Pedro's whistle, or Mr. Ravelini's, would bring him back. Ha! That would teach the stupid boy to think he knew such a lot, and could manage the dogs.

"Come on," he said impatiently. "We must go. You'll have to tell Mr. Ravelini you've lost a dog. My word, he *will* be furious!"

CHAPTER FIVE

BOUNCER IS VERY CLEVER

THEY went back to the circus. Dick turned round every now and again to see whether Tinker was racing after them, but he wasn't. The boy was very upset. He felt quite sure that Larry had unloosed the dog—but how could he say that to Mr. Ravelini? He hadn't *seen* Larry doing it!

"You'd better go and tell Mr. Ravelini straight away," said Larry spitefully, as they went into the field gate. "Go on! I'll put the dogs away."

Dick went to find Mr. Ravelini, but he was nowhere in the field. So the boy went to the blue and yellow caravan. Pedro was there, of course, but there was no one else. He was pleased to see Dick.

"Hallo!" he called. "Did you have a good run? I say! Whatever's the matter? You look as miserable as a wet hen!"

"I feel it, too," said Dick. "I've lost Tinker. He slipped away when Larry and I were having a rest. I didn't see him go."

"I say!" said Pedro in alarm. "Uncle will be pretty wild. I bet Larry loosed him, Dick, just to spite you! What a beast he is!"

"Where's your uncle?" asked Dick. "I'll have to tell him."

"He's gone to the town to arrange about the opening of the show tomorrow," said Pedro. "He'll be back in an hour or two. I say—I've got an idea!"

"What?" asked poor Dick.

"Can't you send your Bouncer to look for Tinker?" asked Pedro. "I've heard that those old sheep dogs are too clever for anything. They can find lost sheep and bring them home, even if there is snow on the ground. Why don't you send him to look for Tinker?"

"He'd never find him," said Dick. But Pedro got Bouncer on to the bed, and began talking to him earnestly, looking into his eyes all the while, and making curious noises every now and again. There was no doubt that Pedro could get inside a dog's mind as well as inside his heart!

"Go find him!" commanded Pedro, pushing Bouncer off the bunk at last. "Go find Tinker. Bring him, bring him, good dog!"

Bouncer wagged his tail and shot off. Dick watched him in astonishment. Bouncer flew through the field gate and shot off to the hills.

"Did he really understand?" he said.

"Every word," said Pedro. "My goodness, Dick, if Bouncer was my dog, wouldn't I teach him a lot! That dog's just longing to learn—but he's too old now. You want a young dog, you know—and even then, only the clever ones. It's a waste of time to teach a stupid dog, and it only makes him unhappy. Only the clever, eager animals should be taught, and they must be taught by kindness."

Dick listened to Pedro talking. He loved hearing about circus ways. He listened until Mrs. Dooly brought them some sandwiches for their dinner, and a tin of pineapple chunks with cream.

"You do have nice meals," said Dick, opening the tin. "I'm jolly hungry, too. I say, did the doctor come this morning, Pedro?"

"Yes," said Pedro. "And my legs are much better. Another two weeks and I'll be all right. I can try and walk next week. You shall help me, Dick."

As they were eating their meal, Larry's face appeared at the door. "Ravelini's coming!" he said. "You're in for it now, Dick!"

Sure enough, Mr. Ravelini came up the steps and entered the caravan. He smiled at the boys.

"Any pineapple left?" he asked. Then he saw Dick's red, unhappy face.

"What's the matter?" he said.

Then Pedro said a funny thing. "Nothing's the matter!" he said. "Nothing at all! Look out of the door, Dick! There's your dog back again—with a friend!"

Dick looked out—and, my goodness, there was old Bouncer trotting along with Tinker close behind him!

"What's Tinker doing out there, loose?" cried Mr. Ravelini?"

"Go and put him away, Dick," said Pedro. "I'll tell Uncle what has happened."

Dick slipped down the steps joyfully. He was so very glad to see Tinker safely back. He took the dog to the big clean cage and put him in. Then he picked up Bouncer and hugged him. He hugged him so hard that Bouncer gasped for breath and squeaked.

"You sound like a mouse!" said Dick putting him down. "Oh, you clever, clever dog! You're better than any circus dog in the world!"

Pedro told Mr. Ravelini what he thought had happened. He knew that Dick would not tell tales of Larry, but he wanted his uncle to know that he, Pedro, felt quite certain it was Larry's fault. So Mr. Ravelini said very little to Dick when he came back with Bouncer.

"It must not happen again," he said. "When you are in charge of anything, it should always be under your eye, Dick. You understand?"

"Yes, sir," said Dick.

"Now come with me and give a hand with the big tent," said Mr. Ravelini. Dick followed him obediently. He passed Larry on the way, and that spiteful fellow was most astonished to see the ring-master being friendly to Dick. He had not seen Tinker come back with Bouncer.

For the rest of that day Dick was too busy to see Pedro for more than a few minutes. He was a strong boy, and very useful at fetching and carrying. It was a big job to get up the circus tent and put the red plush ring inside, and the benches for the people to sit on. Curtains had to be arranged at one side of the ring, where the performers entered, and the trapezes for the three acrobats had to be put up, with steel ladders to reach them.

Dick helped Mr. Roony. He helped Madame Sara when she wanted her monkeys' bicycles taken into the ring for a practice. Each of her monkeys had her own bicycle, and it was most amusing to see them riding round and round the ring at top speed.

"Wendy can ride without touching her handle-bars!" said Madame Sara proudly. "Wendy! Get on and show Dick what you can do!"

Wendy leapt on to her saddle and put her small feet on to the tiny pedals. She raced round the ring, ringing her bell. Then she folded her small arms and rode without using the handle-bars. Dick thought she was marvellous.

But when another monkey, Lulie, tried to do the same, Wendy was jealous. She rode straight at Lulie and tipped her off her bicycle, and then, when Madame Sara scolded her, she tore up the steel ladder and leapt to one of the swinging trapezes in the roof. There she sat, chattering away to herself.

"Oh, you really are a wicked creature!" cried Madame Sara. "Come down at once, Wendy!" But Wendy wouldn't. So Madame Sara had to send Dick to buy some grapes. As soon as the naughty monkey saw Madame Sara giving grapes to the other monkeys, she came flying down for her share.

"And you just won't have any, you tiresome child!" cried Madame Sara to her monkey. "You will go to your basket and stay there by yourself."

So Wendy went off to her basket in Madame Sara's caravan, and had to wait half an hour for the grapes she loved.

Dick was tired at the end of the day. He was hungry, too. It was such a hot evening that Mr.

Ravelini carried Pedro from his bunk on to the grass, where he had spread a rug. "We will eat round a camp fire tonight," said the ringmaster.

So they sat out there in the summer twilight, round a glowing fire that Mr. Ravelini had made, and on which Mrs. Dooly had cooked a most delicious stew for them. Dick was almost asleep. Charlie the clown was playing his concertina softly, and somewhere at the other end of the field the six bandsmen were practising a tune. They did not look like bandsmen, for they still wore their grooms' clothes. They all helped with the horses, and played for the show when it was open.

"Get to bed now," said Mr. Ravelini. "Come on, Pedro." He lifted the boy up into his arms and carried him into the caravan. Dick almost fell up the steps after him, he was so tired. Bouncer leapt up, too. He was never tired!

"I'll just go round and see that the dogs and the horses are all right," said the ringmaster—and by the time that he came back, the boys were so fast asleep that they didn't even hear him!

CHAPTER SIX

DICK GETS A TREAT—AND A SHOCK!

NEXT day there was a great bustle, for the show was to open that evening. Madame Sara finished the new coats for her monkeys. Mr. Roony bought a new cricket bat for his two elephants. They played cricket marvellously in the ring, and once Pal had hit a ball right into the very back row of the watching audience!

"I wish I was going into the ring," said Pedro gloomily. "Larry takes my place with the dogs, but he's no good. He helps Mr. Ravelini. You'd better go and see the show tonight, Dick. You'll like it now you know everyone.

So Dick, in great excitement, went to see the show. He went behind the big curtain and watched all the performers getting ready to go into the ring for the grand parade. He hardly knew them!

"Is that really Madame Sara?" wondered Dick, as he saw a handsome woman, dressed in a wonderful sparkling frock, go by him, leading her five monkeys in their new coats. It *was* Madame Sara, looking as grand as a queen.

Mr. Ravelini was magnificent in a brilliant red coat, a shining top hat, spotless white riding breeches, black top boots, and the biggest, longest whip that Dick had ever seen.

"Crack!" went the whip, and all the performers hurried to take their places. The bandsmen were already in their seats, looking very fine indeed in red and black uniforms.

Mr. Roony was dressed in white velvet, with a short red cloak that sparkled with sequins. He looked so fine that Dick hardly dared speak to him. The elephants were beside him, glad to go into the ring, for they loved a crowd of people.

Up came Philippo, Yosif, and Bella the three acrobats in pink tights that glittered as they moved. They wore tight-fitting helmets with enormous red feathers. They smiled at Dick. Charlie the clown grinned at him, too. They all liked the boy, for he didn't grumble at anything and was always ready to help.

Charlie was in his clown's suit again, and his strangely painted red and white face looked very comical. He had stuck enormous black eyebrows on, which went up and down all the time. Dick began to laugh at him—but Ravelini's whip cracked again. The band struck up a gay marching tune. The horses were brought up, and the ringmaster leapt on to the back of his own beautiful black mare, Sally.

The other horsemen sprang to their saddles, too. They were dressed in Russian suits, with loose white silk blouses, braided fur hats, red silk trousers, and big boots.

There was a long, loud roll on the big drum—"Rr-rr-r-rr-rr!" The great curtains were swung back—and in rode the circus parade!

The horses trotted slowly round the ring, holding their proud heads high, with their nodding feathers. In leapt the three supple acrobats, and in trotted Charlie the clown, his ridiculous eyebrows going up and down. He turned cartwheels and somersaults and shouted funny jokes all the time. How the people laughed at him!

Soon the whole circus parade was in the ring, and Dick wished he was one of them! How fine they looked! How clever they were!

He went to a seat at the back, and watched the show from beginning to end. He loved the two clever elephants playing cricket with their keeper. He thought the five monkeys were marvellous, and he was thrilled at the way they rode their bicycles, had their dinner with cups and dishes and plates, and even put themselves to bed in a little cot!

The horses danced round in time to the music. Every time that Mr. Ravelini cracked his whip, the band changed its tune and the horses did a different step. Then four clever riders did tricks on four horses, standing up, jumping from one horse to another, till Dick was quite muddled with seeing them.

Charlie the clown made him laugh till he cried.

The silly things he did, and the times he fell over! He thought that Charlie and the eight dogs were the two cleverest turns in the circus.

Mr. Ravelini and Larry had the dogs between them. Larry looked fine in a red suit with a white cloak. The eight dogs, happy and eager, showed off all the things they could do, and sat on their own stools each time the whip cracked. The great turn of the evening was when Leppi was put into a big wooden train with pedals for his feet. Off went Leppi, driving the engine round the ring at great speed!

"That's Pedro's own trick," thought Dick. "Larry can bow all he likes—but it was Pedro who taught Leppi that!"

He slipped out of his seat to give the dogs a good feed when they came out of the ring. They were always well rewarded, and looked forward eagerly to their meal.

The dogs crowded round him, their coats white and smooth, their eyes bright. Leppi had quite recovered from Larry's blow, but she would not go near Larry now if she could help it. It was so unusual for anyone in the circus to be cruel to an animal that Leppi had had a shock.

All the people went out of the tent, chattering and laughing. It had been a good show. Much money had been taken and Mr. Ravelini was pleased. It meant good pay for everyone when the circus did well. It was to stay for three nights and then move on again. It never stayed anywhere for long, but was always on the move.

Dick locked the dogs up in their cage and drew up

the side, leaving open the ventilating windows. The dogs went to their straw happily, tired and full-fed. Dick went to Pedro's caravan.

"It's the finest show I ever saw!" he said to Pedro. "I loved it. Oh, hurry up and get your legs right, Pedro—I do want to see *you* in the ring with the dogs!"

The next two days went quickly. Dick looked after the dogs well, and cleaned out their cage so thoroughly that Mrs. Dooly said he would make a fortune as a charwoman! Pedro's legs were much better. The doctor said that he might try a little walk soon. Dick was glad for Pedro, but sad when he thought that his stay with the circus would come to an end.

"And then what shall I do?" thought the boy. "Just tramp round the country again, I suppose."

Dick had a shock on the third night of the show. He was in the circus field, watching the people come in through the gate, paying as they came, when he saw a face he knew.

Dick stared, and his heart began to beat fast. It was Mr. Harris, the head of the Home that Dick had run away from! With him was Mrs. Harris, his wife, who did all the cooking for the Home.

Dick saw Mrs. Harris staring at him—and then she suddenly pulled hard at her husband's arm. Dick felt sure she knew him! He ducked down, ran behind a caravan, crawled under a cart, squeezed through the hedge, and crouched there, trembling. Suppose they looked for him—or even asked for him?

"I *can't* go back," said Dick to himself. He felt something by his foot and looked down. It was

Bouncer—and old Bouncer was also crouching down as if he didn't want to be seen!

"So you've seen Mr. Harris, too," whispered Dick. "Poor old Bouncer! You know they'd take you away from me if they found us!"

Dick peered through the hedge. Mr. and Mrs. Harris had gone into the circus tent. He ran round to the tent and went behind the big curtains that hung down at the entrance to the ring. He peeped through a hole. Yes—Mr. Harris was in the second row opposite, with Mrs. Harris by his side. They hadn't come to fetch him—they had come to see the circus.

But supposing they had seen him? They would certainly ask about him—perhaps come back the next day! Thank goodness, the circus was on the move tomorrow.

"It's going early, too," thought Dick. "What a good thing! Bouncer, come here—don't you dare to go away from me tonight! I don't want Mr. Harris to see you, or he'd know you at once."

When Dick had put the dogs away safely that night, he ran to tell Pedro what had happened. Mr. Ravelini had gone to put his horses away, and the two boys had ten minutes alone. Dick poured out all his fears.

"Do you think they really saw you?" asked Pedro.

"Mrs. Harris did, I'm sure," said Dick. "Oh, do you think I'll be found and taken back?"

"No; just you see that you're *not* found!" said Pedro. "Keep a good lookout, and if you see anyone coming to hunt for you, you just hide yourself, and Bouncer, too. Once we're away from here you'll be safe."

"All right," said Dick. "It's a good thing Larry doesn't know about me—I guess he'd tell tales if he could. He can't imagine how we got Tinker back the other day."

"There's my uncle," said Pedro. "Talk about something else."

Mr. Ravelini came in, tired and rather cross.

"Now, now!" he said. "Didn't I tell you two boys to settle in early tonight, and go to sleep? We start off at six o'clock tomorrow. Lie down, Pedro, at once and don't let me hear another word."

"No, sir," muttered the two boys, and there was silence. But Dick was thinking in delight, "Ah, *six* o'clock! Nobody will come for me before then! I'll be safely away with the circus long before anybody comes.!"

CHAPTER SEVEN

THE CIRCUS GOES ON THE ROAD

NEXT morning, what a bustle there was! Mr. Ravelini woke Dick up just before six o'clock. The sun was already shining from a blue sky. Mrs. Dooly brought two steaming hot cups of tea to the caravan, and Pedro, who woke just then, demanded one for himself, too.

"You're not doing any work, Pedro," said Mr. Ravelini, with a twinkle in his eye. "You don't need a cup of tea!"

But Pedro had plans. He meant to sit at the door of the caravan and keep a good lookout in case Mr. and Mrs. Harris should happen to come early. He was going to do a spot of work, too.

"I want to sit and see everyone getting ready to

go," he told Mr. Ravelini. "Will you help me to the door, Uncle?"

So Ravelini helped him to the door and then went off to oversee everything. Pedro winked at Dick. "I'm on guard for you!" he said. "You go and help all you can, Dick. Don't worry. I'll whistle like this"—Pedro gave a piercing whistle—"if I see anyone strange about." Dick grinned.

"Well, I shall be able to hear *that* all right!" he said, going down the steps. "Goodbye—I'll go and help now. I told Philippo I'd help him to pack up his trapezes and ladders."

Off he went, and soon he was very busy indeed, roping together all the acrobats' belongings, giving Madame Sara a hand with her caravan, which was drawn by one of the circus horses. All Ravelini's own beautiful black horses that danced so well in the ring were led off in a line together, and did not draw any vans. Only the great broad-backed horses that the performers stood and jumped on were allowed to draw the cars and vans.

The big tent was taken down and stacked into a great van. How hard everyone worked! How they shouted and laughed together in the early morning sun! Dick enjoyed every minute, and could not imagine why Larry grumbled so much.

"He must be lazy," thought Dick. "I never heard anyone do so much grumbling!"

"Hie, Larry!" yelled Mr. Ravelini. "Don't you forget those pails down by the stream! Put them in the little red cart!"

Larry turned a sulky face to the ringmaster, but did not dare to say anything.

"I don't see why *you* can't go and get those pails," he muttered to Dick as he passed him. "You're such a busy little bee, aren't you!"

"All right, I'll get them if you like," said Dick, who didn't mind doing anything. But Larry scowled at him.

"Don't you dare to fetch them!" he said. "You know that would get me into trouble with Mr. Ravelini—and that's just what you'd like, isn't it?"

"Of course not," said Dick. "But get them yourself if you feel like that!"

Pedro sat at the door of the blue and yellow caravan, keeping a sharp watch on the road. Nobody came down it except an early milkman and the postman. Time went on. Seven o'clock. Eight o'clock. Ravelini grew impatient.

He cracked his big whip. Everyone flew to their caravan or cart. They knew that the circus must be on the road in a few minutes now. Mr. Roony had his elephants ready. The horses were already in the lane, stamping their feet and nodding their magnifiicent black heads. Madame Sara was driving her caravan out of the field gate herself, her monkeys safely locked inside.

"They're peeping out of the window like small brown-faced children!" said Dick, as the caravan passed him. "What fun they must have!"

"Hie, boy!" shouted Mr. Ravelini. "Can you drive my caravan for me? There's one of my horses that is troublesome this morning and I'd like to be with her. I don't want Larry to drive the van—he and Pedro are always scrapping."

"Well, sir, I'd love to drive it," said Dick, his face

red with pleasure. "But I've never driven a horse before."

"Uncle, Uncle! Put me on the seat beside Dick, and I can help him to drive!" yelled Pedro from the door of the caravan.

So Ravelini put Pedro beside Dick, and Pedro showed his friend how to hold the reins.

"Old Blossom takes our van," he said, "and she doesn't really need anyone to drive her—she knows exactly what to do. Look—hold the reins so."

The whole circus moved slowly out of the field. The elephants trumpeted impatiently. They loved their walk from town to town. The horses neighed. All the dogs leapt and barked for joy when they felt their cage moving. Bouncer barked back. He sat beside Dick in the driving seat, the proudest dog in the world. It was a squash with the three of them, but they didn't mind a bit.

Down the road went the circus procession. Charlie the clown drove his own little red caravan, and sang songs at the top of his voice. He always loved a move.

"Well," said Pedro to Dick, as they moved off at last, "you're safe! Nobody came!"

"Thank goodness!" said Dick. "It was decent of you to watch out for me, Pedro."

The circus went through the big town on its way to its next camping-place. Some of the townspeople, who had seen the circus performing, came out to wave goodbye.

"Come again!" they shouted, and Mr. Ravelini raised his shiny top hat and bowed. Charlie took off his cap, stood up and bowed too, just as if *he*

Coming towards them was Mr. Harris

were the ringmaster. That made everyone laugh.

"He was the clown!" said somebody. "Three cheers for old Charlie!"

Just as they were half-way through the town, Dick clutched Pedro by the arm and went pale. "Pedro! There's Mr. Harris!"

Sure enough, coming smartly towards them down the road, was Mr. Harris, looking with interest at the circus. Charlie chose to stand on his hands on his driving-seat just then, and Mr. Harris stopped to watch him.

"Quick! Give me the reins!" said Pedro at once. "Jump down the other side and hide somewhere, Dick, don't hide in the caravan—if he's come to look for you, every one of them will be searched."

Dick pushed the reins into Pedro's hands and jumped down. He ran into a side road and dodged behind a wall there. It was a builder's yard, but nobody was there.

Dick's heart was beating fast. He found a chink between a pile of boards stacked up beside the wall and looked through it. Would Mr. Harris stop the circus and demand that Mr. Ravelini should give him up? Well—they wouldn't find him in the circus! He'd soon run off to the countryside again!

He saw something that puzzled him very much. A big green bus came rumbling down the street, going the opposite way of the circus. Mr. Harris hailed it, and jumped in. Off went the bus, carrying him the opposite way!

Dick watched the bus turn a corner and then he tore after the circus procession. He soon caught it up, for it did not go fast. He climbed up beside Pedro.

"Did you see?" panted Dick. "He caught a bus! He didn't stop and see if I was with the circus. Isn't it funny? I *know* Mrs. Harris saw me last night."

Pedro thought hard as he gave the reins to Dick. "Well," he said at last, "I think I know what's happened, Dick. You were seen last night in the circus field, but that didn't mean to say you were *with* the circus. I expect that the Harrises think you just went to see it, and are hiding somewhere about there, in a haystack or something. They didn't imagine you would be moving off with us!"

"Yes—you're right," said Dick, excited. "Oh, Pedro, that means I'm safe! They'll hunt for me out there around the circus field, and they won't find me! And by that time we'll be safely away to our next camp."

"Don't be too sure," said Pedro. "We'll just go on keeping a good lookout till we really feel you're safe."

It was fun travelling along that day. All the people in the villages they passed came out to see them and to wave to them. Madame Sara went into her caravan and brought out Wendy, who sat beside her, holding the reins in a very important way, making everyone laugh. She really was a very clever little monkey.

They stopped for dinner on a big common. The two boys were so hungry that they could hardly wait for their meal. Mrs. Dooly cooked it in her own caravan and brought it to them. Mr. Ravelini went to an inn to have his, so the boys had theirs alone together. Mr. Ravelini had lifted Pedro down to the grass, and he sprawled happily beside Dick.

They ate fried bacon, sausages and eggs, and finished up with some tinned peaches. "That was fine!" said Dick with a sigh. "Look, there's an ice-cream man! Got any money, Pedro? I haven't even a ha'penny!"

"Yes, I think I've got some," said Pedro, who, like all the circus folk, was never very sure what money he had or hadn't. He looked in his pockets and brought out a shilling.

"Oooh!" said Dick. "Good! I'll go and get ice-creams for both of us."

"Get one for Bouncer and one for Wendy!" shouted Pedro. So Dick got four ice-creams. He took one to Wendy. She held out her little paw for it eagerly. She simply *loved* ice-cream! She was soon eating it, whilst Madame Sara looked on and laughed at her.

Bouncer was greedy over his. Two bites and it was gone—then he sat and looked pleadingly at the boys, hoping for a bit of theirs. But they wouldn't give him any. "No, Bouncer," said Dick. "You shouldn't have gobbled yours up so quickly. Now you just sit and watch us eating ours!"

"Look, Dick, look at the elephants," said Pedro with a giggle. "They've gone to get ice-creams too!"

Sure enough they had. All the animals loved ice-cream, and Chum and Pal were just as greedy over them as Bouncer. Mr. Roony had taken his two elephants to buy a shilling ice-cream each, for a treat, as it was such a very hot day.

Chum knew quite well where the ice-cream was kept—under the round lid on the cart. With his trunk he politely took off the lid for the surprised ice-cream man, and held it up in the air. Pal was just about to put in his trunk for the ice-creams when Mr. Roony stopped him.

"Pal!" he said. And Pal took his trunk away and swung it from side to side. He was very obedient.

The ice-cream man handed out two big ice-creams. Chum was about to put back the lid, when he changed his mind and put it solemnly on the top of the ice-cream man's head, like a hat.

Dick and Pedro roared with laughter. "That's the funniest elephant I've ever seen," said Pedro. "Look at them with their ice-creams, Dick!"

Mr. Roony undid the paper from the ice-creams, and the two elephants took them. They put them carefully into their mouths, and stood there enjoying them. The ice-cream man watched in wonder.

"Coo!" he said. "I wish I had customers like those elephants every day! I would make a fortune!"

Mr. Ravelini came round the dinner camp, bidding everyone get ready to move again. He looked at each cart to make sure that everything was safe, and that no rope was slipping. Dick went with him to help.

The ringmaster came to the little red cart that carried the odds and ends. He lifted the tarpaulin cover and looked inside. He turned to Dick.

"Were the water pails put in?" he asked.

"I don't know, sir," said Dick.

"I can't see them here," said Ravelini. "They're important—we water the horses with those, and we can't do without them. I wonder where Larry put them."

He glanced round. Larry was lying under a bush, his cap over his eyes. Ravelini shouted loudly: "Larry! Where are the pails?"

Larry sat up. His face went red. "Er—aren't they there, sir?" he asked.

Mr. Ravelini flew into a rage. "You know very well they're not here!" he yelled. "Did you leave them behind?"

Larry didn't know what to say. He didn't dare to say he had forgotten them—and yet if he said he had remembered them, the ringmaster would ask him where they were. So he stood there, looking foolish and saying nothing.

Ravelini caught him by the shoulders and shook him till his teeth rattled. "Lazy, good-for-nothing fellow!" he roared. "So you have left those good pails behind after all I said to you! I've a good mind to take my whip to you!"

"Please, sir, I'll go back for them," mumbled Larry, frightened. "I'll take the cart and go back. I can drive quickly, and I'll catch you up before nightfall."

Ravelini gave him a push that sent him flying into a gorse bush. "You'd *better* get them!" he said. "Go on—take the cart at once. Drive back to the field—and it will be bad for you if you find someone else has taken those pails! Join us again tonight, you tiresome boy."

He turned on his heel and stamped back to his horse, red with rage. Dick was too afraid to go with him. Larry picked himself up out of the bush and looked at his scratches, where the gorse had pricked him. "I suppose *you* told Mr. Ravelini I'd forgotten the pails?" he said, and he aimed a kick at Dick.

Dick jumped aside. "I did *not*!" he said. "I don't tell tales."

Larry sprang up into the driving-seat of the little red cart, his face sulky. He turned it round and drove off smartly in the direction from which they had just come. Dick went to tell Pedro.

"Serve him jolly well right," said Pedro with a laugh. "He'll have to do a good day's work for a change. His arms will be sore with driving tonight. I guess he will be blue when he gets back."

But Larry wasn't blue! He drove back that night looking cheerful and spiteful. What could have happened to make him so pleased?

CHAPTER EIGHT

A STRANGE HIDING-PLACE

It wasn't long before the boys found out. As soon as the camp was settling into its new field, Larry came round to their caravan.

"So he's a boy from a Home, is he!" said the spiteful lad, grinning all over his face. "So somebody's looking for him, is he? Well, it won't be long before you're found now, Dick."

"What do you mean?" asked Dick in dismay, looking at Larry from where he sat on the steps of the blue-and-yellow caravan.

"Just what I say!" said Larry. "Aha! When I got back to the field I found a friend of yours there—and he happened to ask me if I knew of any strange boy called Dick. So I was able to help him quite a lot."

"You spiteful—horrid—hateful——" began Pedro, who had heard everything. Larry grinned, waved his hand, and disappeared. Dick was miserable. Now things were indeed bad.

Pedro could hardly speak for rage. He bounced up and down on his bunk, he almost burst with trying to find bad enough things to say about Larry. At last he calmed down, and the two boys discussed everything together.

"Well, Mr. Harris will certainly come here now," said Dick gloomily. "What do you think I'd better do, Pedro? Slip away from the circus whilst there's still time—or give myself up, and let them take Bouncer away from me for good?"

"You jolly well won't do either!" said Pedro. "You'll hide here in the circus—yes, you will! I'll hide you! And you can stay hidden till Mr. Harris thinks you've gone—and then I'll tell my uncle everything and get him to send Larry away, and keep you on instead!"

"Oh, Pedro, you're a good sort," said Dick, thumping the boy on the shoulder. "But you might get into trouble for hiding me—and anyway, I don't think Mr. Ravelini would keep me."

"Sh! Here comes my uncle," said Pedro. "We won't say anything in front of him. We'll plan things when he's asleep. No one will come searching here before tomorrow. We've heaps of time."

Ravelini told them that Larry had found the pails and brought them back. "That boy is no use," he grumbled. "I wish I'd never told his father I'd give him a chance here."

"Why did you take Larry, Uncle?" asked Pedro.

"I took him because his father couldn't manage him at home," said the ringmaster, "and he thought the hard, rough life of a circus would do him good. Larry's father once did me a good turn —so I took the boy for him. But he's a bad lot—lazy, untruthful, spiteful. Not the right sort for a circus at all.

"Uncle," said Pedro, "I want to try and walk again. The doctor said I could try soon, didn't he— and my legs do feel so much better. Look what I can do with them!"

Pedro lay on his bunk and waggled his legs in the air as if he were riding a bicycle upside down. Ravelini laughed.

"Good gracious!" he said. "There certainly doesn't look much wrong. All right. Come along down the steps and we'll see what happens."

He lifted the boy down the steps, and then, with Dick holding one arm and his uncle holding the other, Pedro staggered along. His face was white, for his legs pained him after being so long unused. But he stuck it, and walked right to the dogs' cage. He looked inside. The dogs barked a welcome at him, and tried their best to get out to him.

"Now let me try to walk alone," said Pedro. They let go his arms and the boy staggered a few steps and then fell to the ground.

"You must go slowly," said Ravelini gently. "Not too much at a time!" He picked Pedro up in his enormous arms and took him back to the caravan. Then he left him to go and see to the horse that had been troublesome.

"What did you want to try and walk alone for when your legs are not ready?" said Dick.

"I had a reason," said Pedro. "You'll see what it is tonight, Dick! I'm going to hide you in a very good place—and I'll have to take you there, and walk back by myself. So I had to try my legs."

"You're a good sport, Pedro," said Dick, thinking that he had indeed found a good friend in trouble.

That night the whole camp was very tired and went to bed early. Even the elephants slept quickly. Mr. Ravelini threw himself on to his bunk, and told the boys that there was not to be a single word spoken.

But they disobeyed him—for as soon as the ring-master began to snore, the boys whispered together.

"You'd better come with me now," said Pedro. "The moon will be up soon and we don't want anyone to see us. Leave Bouncer here."

Pedro managed to creep from his bunk to the floor. Dick helped him down the steps. Then, half carrying him, he let Pedro lead him to his hiding-place.

Pedro went to the dogs' cage! He unlocked the door and at once all the dogs hurled themselves on to him in joy—but not one sound did they make! At a single whispered word from Pedro they had all known that they must be completely silent.

Pedro had a torch with him. He shone it round the cage. At the back, tucked into a corner, was a big kennel.

"That's where we put any dog who is not well," explained Pedro. "Well, Dick, my idea is this—that I put Leppi there—with *you*! It's a good big kennel, and we can fill it well with straw. You can get to the back and hide in the straw—and Leppi can lie at the front. See?"

"Well!" said Dick in the greatest astonishment. "What an idea! I should never have thought of that! It's a fine big kennel—I can easily get into it."

"You needn't get in it till about six," said Pedro. "But you'd better sleep somewhere near it so that you can pop in at once. The straw is kept in that cart over there."

Dick got the straw. He put some into the kennel and then crawled in himself to see how much room there was. There was plenty! He could sit at the back quite comfortably.

"You must take Leppi in with you when you go," said Pedro. "You'll find a chain at the front of the kennel there. Put it on to his collar so that he can't run out too far. Draw back this side-piece of the cage when you go to the kennel so that there is a partition between you and the other dogs. That's what we do when we want to separate any dog here. See—the partition slides out of here quite easily."

Pedro showed Dick how the wooden partition slid across the cage, separating the kennel-place from the rest of the van. Dick nodded. "I see," he said. "I can manage that quite all right. Thanks awfully, Pedro—it's very good of you to take all this trouble for me."

"Well, good night," said Pedro, getting up from the ground, where he had been sitting. "I'll get back. I don't want you to come with me in case Bouncer barks and wakes my uncle. He'll ask me awkward questions then, and perhaps go and look for you. You'd better sleep in that cart where you got the straw from, and pop into the kennel before it gets light."

Pedro staggered away from the dogs' cage. Dick longed to help him, but he knew that Pedro was proud and wanted to go alone. The boy went to the cart from which he had taken the straw and got into it. The straw was warm. He was soon fast asleep.

He awoke when the sun was rising. The camp was perfectly quiet. Dick got cautiously out of the cart and went to the dogs' cage. He undid it and slipped inside. He picked up Leppi, and went to the kennel. He pulled the partition quietly across and then fastened the chain on to Leppi's collar.

Then he crept to the back of the kennel and pulled the straw over him.

Leppi was rather surprised at first, but after a few words from Dick she lay down at the entrance to the kennel, put her head on her paws,and slept.

Dick slept too, his head nodding on his chest. He awoke when the elephants trumpeted as Mr. Roony took them down to the stream for a drink. He wondered where he was at first—and then he remembered. Of course! He was in the dogs' kennel!

"I hope I'm not found," thought Dick, as he felt in his pocket for some bread and cheese that Pedro had thoughtfully given him. "If only Mr. Harris doesn't come!"

But Mr. Harris *did* come—with a policeman too!

CHAPTER NINE

THE HUNT FOR DICK

THAT morning, when Mr. Ravelini awoke, he missed Dick, but thought that he had gone to see to the dogs. So he said nothing at first. But when Pedro and he began their breakfast, brought to them by old Mrs. Dooly, he spoke to Pedro.

"Where is Dick?"

"I expect he is with the dogs," answered Pedro, quite truthfully.

"Wasn't he here when you woke up this morning?" asked Ravelini.

"No, Uncle, he wasn't," said Pedro.

"Go and call him, Mrs. Dooly," said Ravelini. "He can finish his jobs after breakfast."

But very soon Mrs. Dooly came back and said that

Dick was not to be found anywhere. Ravelini grunted.

"He's about somewhere," he said, eating his breakfast. "Well, he'll come when he's hungry."

Pedro was feeling excited. When would his uncle discover that Dick was not to be found—and when would Mr. Harris come?

"Uncle, can I walk about the caravan today?" said Pedro. "My legs do feel so much better."

"Yes, you may," said Ravelini. "But don't go outside. I'm not going to have you falling down the steps."

When his uncle had gone to see to his horses, Pedro sat himself at the door of the caravan to watch. He wondered how Dick was getting on. Somehow or other he must manage to get some food to him during the day.

He was wondering how he could do this, when he suddenly saw something that made his heart jump. There was a man at the field gate—with a policeman!

"It's Mr. Harris," said Pedro to himself. "And oh, my goodness, he's got a policeman with him. Oh dear—I don't like it. Suppose they find Dick? What will happen to him? And will they punish me, too, for hiding him?"

The boy felt afraid, but he made up his mind that he would not give Dick away. He would not tell them where his friend was hiding, no matter how many times they asked him.

Mr. Harris spoke to Yosif, and Yosif waved his hand to where Mr. Ravelini was talking to a groom. "There he is," Pedro heard Yosif say in his clear voice. "*He's* our ringmaster. Ask him what you want to know."

All the circus folk stared in surprise at the sight of a stranger with a policeman—all but Larry. He wasn't surprised at all. He was pleased. He went across to Pedro.

"Your friend Dick won't like his visitors this morning, will he?" he said, with a spiteful grin.

"I don't want to talk to you," said Pedro in disgust. "You're about the meanest fellow I've ever seen. Go and put yourself in somebody's dustbin—that's the right place for you!"

Larry scowled. He did not dare to hit Pedro. "You wait till your uncle knows about Dick," he said. "You'll get into hot water too."

"It's a pity *you* don't get into hot water a bit oftener!" said Pedro sharply. "You'd be a bit cleaner then!"

Ravelini was talking to Mr. Harris. He looked worried. He came over to the blue and yellow caravan with Mr. Harris and the policeman.

"Pedro," he said "did you know that Dick had run away from the Home where he had been put?"

"Yes, Uncle," said Pedro. "He didn't want to be parted from Bouncer. You know how he loves him—just like we love our dogs! He told me that he couldn't give Bouncer up—so he ran away with him."

"Well, he's got to come back," said Mr. Harris. "And I've brought this policeman with me to help me to look for him. He has authority to search the whole camp."

"Where *is* Dick?" said Mr. Ravelini. "I haven't seen him this morning."

"Neither have I," said Pedro truthfully.

"There's his dog!" said Mr. Harris, pointing to

Bouncer, who was poking his nose out beside Pedro at the door of the caravan. "Is he in that caravan?"

"We'd better start the search, sir," said the policeman. "Stand aside, young fellow. We'll begin here first."

Pedro stood aside. The policeman searched the caravan quickly, but there was no one there except Pedro and Bouncer.

"We'll go to the next caravan," said the policeman. So off they went to Madame Sara, who was most indignant at having strangers in her caravan.

"Upsetting my monkeys!" she said angrily. Wendy chattered at the tall policeman, and then jumped nimbly to the top of his helmet. From there he jumped to Mr. Harris's shoulder, which made him yell with fright. He could not bear animals.

"Take it off, take it off!" he shouted. But the more frightened he became, the more Wendy clung to him, nibbling his ear and pinching his cheek.

Madame Sara laughed. She took Wendy from the frightened man, and it wasn't long before he was safely outside the caravan!

"I don't go into any more vans," he told the policeman, feeling his ear tenderly. "Goodness knows what we might find in this circus!"

"Oh, it's a good circus," answered the policeman, who was getting tired of Mr. Harris. "Mr. Ravelini is a kind master, and all the animals here are well treated and happy."

Pedro and Ravelini watched the two men searching the circus. Ravelini turned to his nephew and looked at him.

"Do you know where Dick is?" he asked.

"Yes, Uncle," answered Pedro, going red.

"Where is he?" asked Ravelini at once.

Pedro was silent. The ringmaster looked at the boy and then clapped him on the shoulder.

"I don't want to know!" he said. "We have to look after our friends, and it seems to me that Dick is not a bad boy. Get back on to the bed, and I'll shut the door and go out. The men have searched our caravan and will not come back to it. If you stay here, they will not ask you awkward questions, and I myself can truthfully say I don't know where he is. But if you have hidden him somewhere in the circus, Pedro, I'm afraid he will be found. The police know well how to search for secret places."

Pedro gave his uncle's arm a grateful squeeze. He got on to the bunk, and Ravelini shut the door on him and went out to join Mr. Harris and the policeman.

Every van and cart had been well searched. Larry had joined in the search, anxious that Dick should be found. He could not *imagine* where he was!

"I'll help you," he said to Mr. Harris. "I know every place where he might be hiding."

So the boy showed the two men barrels and boxes in which a boy might hide—but no Dick was there. He helped them to unload the little red cart, thinking that perhaps Dick had managed to wriggle his way underneath the goods there. But no boy was there either.

Mr. Harris came to the dogs' big cage and peered in. Ravelini was there, feeding the dogs and giving them water.

"Any chance of a boy hiding anywhere in this cage?" asked the policeman, peering in.

"Come in and see," said Ravelini. "But be careful of the dog in the kennel there—he's chained up, and may be a bit fierce if he sees that youngster with you. He's not liked you since you ill-treated him the other day, Larry."

Larry looked as black as thunder. He did not want strangers to know he was ill-behaved. Mr. Harris refused at once to go into the big cage. He was afraid of being bitten. He hated dogs, and would allow neither dog nor cat at his Home.

So the policeman went in, and looked round and about the benches in the cage. He slid back the partition that divided the cage in two, and peered in at the big kennel from the other side. Leppi growled angrily. She could see Larry behind the policeman, and she could also smell that Mr. Harris disliked dogs. She bared her teeth and the policeman stepped back hastily.

Poor Dick! He was at the back of the kennel hidden well in the straw. He heard Mr. Harris's voice. He heard the policeman and Larry come into the cage. He trembled, and hoped that Leppi would let no one into the kennel.

"Good dog, good dog!" said the policeman to Leppi, who, with her eye on Larry, was still growling fiercely. He turned to Larry. "Here, boy—you know these dogs better than I do. Get this dog quiet, so that I can search here."

But as soon as Larry drew nearer, Leppi flew out to the length of her short chain, and barked the place down! The other dogs grew restless and began to growl, sniffing round the policeman's legs in a way he didn't like at all. As for Larry, he hopped out of the cage quickly. He knew the warning note in the dogs' snarls, and he wondered why the ringmaster did not quiet them with a word, as he could so easily do.

The policeman decided that he need not do any more hunting there. He stepped out of the cage as quickly as ever he could. Mr. Ravelini shut and locked it, putting the key in his pocket. Dick heard everyone going out and he breathed a little more easily. "Good old Leppi!" he whispered. "Good old Leppi!"

Leppi went inside the kennel and snuggled down beside the boy, all the fur on her neck still standing up straight, for she was quite ready to fly out and bark again if she saw or heard Larry.

Mr. Harris was speaking to the ringmaster. "Well, sir, it seems as if the boy isn't in your circus today," he said. "He must have heard we were coming, and have run away. Perhaps this boy here, who told us about him, warned him and he ran off."

"Oh no, sir, I didn't say a word," said Larry untruthfully.

"He's probably gone off for good," said Mr. Harris. "We must keep our eyes open for him somewhere else. Good day, Mr. Ravelini."

"Good day," said the ringmaster. He waited until they were safely off the field, and then he turned on Larry, who was trying to creep away, for he could see something he didn't like in the ringmaster's eye.

"Look here, my lad!" began Ravelini in a quiet, fierce voice. "There's something wrong with you. Dick's a good, helpful lad, and you've done your best to get him into trouble. You wanted to get him out of the circus—you were afraid he would take your place! Well, let me tell you this—no circus wants a fellow like *you*!"

He caught hold of Larry's shoulder and shook him. "Circus folk stick up for one another. Circus folk treat their animals as one of themselves. Circus folk do their bit for the circus and for each other. But you'll never learn that! You can go back to your father, you miserable fellow! A circus is too good for you!"

He looked as if he would like to give the boy a good whipping, and Larry was frightened. "I don't want to go back to my father," he whined. "He's hard on me."

"Just what you want!" roared Ravelini. "I have a good mind to call back Mr. Harris and tell him he can take you with him!"

"Oh no, sir, please don't!" wept Larry. Mr. Ravelini looked at him in disgust.

"Crying now!" he said. "I'll soon stop that! You go to Philippo and tell him to give you the big pail and the old cloths—and you can wash the wheels of every wagon in the place today! A bit of hard work will do you good!"

Larry went off, sniffing, and wiping his sleeve across his eyes. Nothing was going right. He hated washing the wheels. They got so dirty, and it was an endless job, for there were so many vans and carts in the circus.

Philippo gave him the big pail and the old cloths with a grin.

"Got to get down to a spot of work, have you?" he said. "Serve you right!"

CHAPTER TEN

PEDRO AND LARRY HAVE A FEW WORDS

MEANWHILE, what was happening to poor Dick? He was still in the kennel, which was very stuffy and hot. He was terribly thirsty. But Pedro had not forgotten him.

He got Yosif, who was passing, to lift him down the caravan steps, which his legs still found difficult to manage. Then he staggered off to a man at the gate, who was selling ginger beer. Pedro bought two bottles and went back to the caravan, his legs feeling stronger as he limped along.

The boy stuffed his pockets full of biscuits, a bar of chocolate, and a hunk of bread. Then he went along to the dogs' kennel. Nobody was about. Pedro felt in his pocket for his key. Both his uncle and he had a key to the dogs' cage. Pedro unlocked the cage and the dogs came rushing round him and Bouncer.

Bouncer knew quite well that Dick was in the kennel. He whined as Pedro slid back the partition, and then rushed for the kennel. Leppi growled and stopped him. Into Leppi's doggy mind had come the idea that she was guarding Dick!

"It's all right, Leppi, old girl," said Pedro in his special doggy voice. Leppi lay down on her back and put all her legs into the air, waiting for Pedro to tickle her. But Pedro, after a quick look round to make sure that no one was about, pushed Leppi gently aside and groped in the straw of the kennel.

"Dick!" Here's some food for you, and some ginger beer. Mr. Harris and the policeman have gone. Cheer up! I'll come again when it's safe, but you may have to stay here all day in case Larry sees you. I think Uncle's going to send him away, then you can come out safely, and we'll see Uncle together."

"Thanks, Pedro," said Dick, and he took the food and drink gratefully. The ginger beer cork came out with a pop, and Dick drank from the bottle, thinking that it was the finest drink he had ever had in all his life. Bouncer tried to creep in beside him, but Pedro hauled him out.

"Now don't you give the game away, Bouncer," he said. "Come along! Lie down, Leppi! Guard him, good dog! Guard him."

Leppi barked. Guard him! Yes, she would! Pedro left the cage and staggered back to the caravan, his legs feeling like wood. Larry saw him and laughed at him.

"Got to see to your dogs yourself, now your friend Dick has vanished, haven't you!" he said.

"Well, so long as *you* don't touch my dogs, I don't care," answered Pedro. "You needn't grin like that, Larry. You'll laugh the other side of your face soon. I'm going to beg my uncle to let you go today! I can't bear the sight of you round this circus any longer. I can tell him a few things about you that you won't like."

"What do you mean?" said Larry, his face going pale.

"I mean a lot of things," said Pedro stoutly. "I know who stole the six tins of pineapple that Mrs. Dooly had in her caravan for us. I know who lost the saddle belonging to Black Diamond, Uncle's horse. I know——"

"You just keep things to yourself," said Larry in a fury. "Nosing round, finding out a lot of things that aren't true."

"I shan't keep any of them to myself," said Pedro. "I shall tell Uncle the whole lot—and when he knows that I once saw you ill-treating White Star, the horse he loves the most—well, I wouldn't be in your shoes for anything!"

"I'll pay you back for this," said Larry, and he looked so fierce that Pedro looked round to see if anyone was near to help him if Larry flew at him. Pedro could hold his own at any ordinary time, but with bad legs he could not hope to stand up to Larry.

But Larry did nothing but look fiercely and spitefully at Pedro. "Yes," he said, "I'll pay you back for this!"

“Stuff!” said Pedro, and went into the caravan, climbing the steps with great difficulty. He flung himself down on the bunk and lay there, quite tired out. Ravelini found him there at dinner-time and looked at him in dismay.

‘ ‘You little idiot!” he said. “You look really ill! You’ve been galloping about too much on those legs of yours—you know what’ll happen, don’t you? You’ll make them bad again, and then you’ll have to lie up for weeks—and what shall I do then, with nobody to help me with the dogs? Dick’s gone, Larry’s no use, and the others are far too busy.”

“Uncle,” said Pedro, sitting up, “if Dick comes back, will you please let him stay here? He’s awfully good with animals, and he’d be no end of a help with the dogs.”

“I don’t know, Pedro,” said his uncle gravely. “We’ve only known the boy a little while, and it’s likely he’s just playing up to us to get us to take him on, so that he needn’t go back to a life he hates. I don’t want another Larry on my hands; and though I say I will get rid of Larry, I don’t think I shall, really —I promised his father to give him a year’s chance, and he’s only been with us a few months. I haven’t room for another boy as well as Larry.”

Pedro was so bitterly disappointed that he felt his eyes filling with tears. He turned away to hide them, for Ravelini had no patience with tears. He said no more, for he knew that it was no use just them.

Mrs. Dooly came in with a fine dinner of stew, tomato sauce, bread, tinned pears and cream. When the circus did well, the camp ate like kings. When it did badly, they went without the things they loved best. It had been doing well for weeks, and the circus folk were happy.

"Ooh, what a fine smell!" said Pedro, cheering up, and blinking away the tell-tale tears. He wished that Dick could share in the meal—but he did not dare to tell his uncle where Dick was now. He might give Dick up to Mr. Harris after all!

CHAPTER ELEVEN

LARRY PLANS A REVENGE

THE camp was very busy that afternoon, for the circus was to open that evening. Larry went on and on with his job of washing the wheels, getting hotter and hotter, and feeling more and more angry with Pedro and Ravelini.

"If only I could pay them out!" thought the spiteful boy, as he washed the wheels of the little red cart. "If only I knew where Dick was and could give him away!"

But he didn't know where Dick was. And for a long time he couldn't think of any way in which to pay Pedro and Ravelini out for their rough treatment of him.

The ringmaster passed him, and took no notice of

him. Something fell to the ground as Ravelini strode by. Larry looked to see what it was. If it was money, he'd keep it!

But it wasn't money. It was a key. Larry picked it up and looked at it. It was the key of the dogs' cage!

Larry put it into his pocket and went on with his work. A plan was slowly forming in his mind.

"If I could get the dogs out—and take them out into the hills, and let the whole lot loose!" he thought. "What a punishment that would be for Pedro and his uncle! I'll do it before the performance tonight. When everyone is in their caravans getting ready for the show, I'll unlock the cage and take the dogs with me!"

The boy rejoiced over the trouble and dismay he would cause. "The dogs won't be able to go into the ring if they're rabbiting in the hills!" he thought. "As for that Leppi, I'd like to stuff her down a rabbit hole that she'd never get out of again!"

The show began at seven. At half-past five everyone was either dressing or taking a hasty tea in their caravans. Only old Mrs. Dooly pottered round, stirring a great pan on a fire she had built outside her own caravan.

Larry emptied his pail of water out beside the dogs' cage, whistling. Then, taking the key out of his pocket, he slipped round to the door, unlocked it and went inside. The dogs looked at him, half expecting a meal.

"Hallo!" said Larry in a kindly voice to the watching dogs. "Would you like a walk, a walk, a walk?"

The dogs knew the meaning of that magic word very well indeed. They adored a run, and at once they ran to Larry, pawing his knees and whining with pleasure. They did not like the boy, but they always loved a walk, no matter who took them.

Dick, in the kennel, pricked up his ears in surprise. A walk? At this time of the day when the show was almost opening? What did Larry mean? He soon knew—for Larry, not guessing that Dick was so near, went on talking to the dogs.

"I'll pay that Pedro out for all he's said to me! I'll lose Ravelini's dogs for him all right! Making me wash dirty wheels all day long so that everyone in the circus laughs at me! I'll pay them both out!"

Dick was amazed. Was Larry really going to take the dogs out—and lose them—to pay out Ravelini and Pedro? Would he dare to do such a thing?

"Yes, and when Ravelini misses you, he'll think it's that boy Dick!" said Larry to the dogs. "I shall say that I saw him get into the cage and take you all away!"

Dick's face burned with rage. He did not know what to do. If he came out of the kennel, Larry would see him and go straight to tell Ravelini or Mr. Harris. He crouched there in the kennel, listening. He made up his mind that when Larry came to get Leppi, he would spring out on him and capture him. Perhaps Mr. Ravelini would believe him if he told him all that he had heard Larry say. He could not bear to think of Pedro's dogs being taken away and lost by Larry.

So Dick waited for Larry to get Leppi—but he didn't come! Larry was afraid of Leppi. He did not want to unchain her, for he was afraid that Leppi would bite him again. So he had slipped out of the cage with the other dogs, and going round the back of the big tent, so that no one could see him, he had made for the hedge, where he knew there was a gap.

So, though Dick waited and waited, Larry did not come—he was already squeezing through the hedge. Dick pushed Leppi aside and looked out of the kennel, straws sticking in his hair. Where was Larry?

The cage was empty! Not a dog was there. Only Leppi, still on her chain, whined beside him.

"He's gone!" said Dick. "What shall I do? Shall I call Mr. Ravelini? If I do, there will be no chance of catching Larry, for he will have had such a good start. Oh, what *am* I to do?"

He ran to the door of the cage and looked out over the camp. No one saw him except Mrs. Dooly, who was cleaning her pan. She was too astonished to say a word. Here was the boy who had been hunted for, creeping out of Leppi's kennel!

Dick didn't even notice Mrs. Dooly. He could see that Larry had not gone out of the field gate. Then, far away, he heard the sound of a bark. The dogs were already on the hill.

Dick darted into the cage again and unchained Leppi. "You must help me, Leppi," he said. And then someone else came to help him—Bouncer!

Somehow Bouncer had sensed that Dick was in need of help. He had come straight out of Pedro's caravan window and come tearing along to the cage. Dick was delighted to see him.

With the two dogs at his heels the boy ran round the big tent and made for the gap in the hedge. Mrs. Dooly saw him go, and wondered if she should tell the ringmaster. Oh, wait till he came out of his caravan—that would be time enough. Dick couldn't be caught now, anyway.

Dick went on and on up the hill. He was stiff with crouching for so long in the kennel, and it was good to run. Far in the distance he could see Larry with the dogs. He *must* catch him—he must, he must! He must get the dogs before they all lost themselves rabbiting!

"Whatever will Pedro say when he knows his dogs are gone?" groaned Dick. "He'll be broken-hearted!"

It was Mr. Ravelini who discovered first that the dogs were gone. He went to the cage to get them ready for the show—and found the door open and the dogs gone. Even Leppi was unchained and gone, too! The ringmaster stared as if he could not believe his eyes.

He ran to his caravan and threw open the door. "Pedro!" he shouted. "Have you got the dogs?"

Pedro sat up with a jerk. He had had to rest his legs that afternoon and evening, for the had done too much in the morning. He looked at his uncle in horror.

"The dogs!" he said. "No, of course I haven't got them. What's happened?"

"They've gone," said Ravelini. "And the show starts in an hour! Hie, Mrs. Dooly! Have you seen the dogs?"

"I saw that young Dick coming out of Leppi's kennel," said the old woman. "He'd got Leppi—and I did see another dog, too—so I reckon he'd got the others as well, if they're gone. The young scamp! I'd have told you if I'd thought he'd taken our dogs."

"Oh, Uncle, he can't have done such a thing!"

cried Pedro. "My dogs! Uncle, Dick couldn't take them!"

At the thought of his precious dogs, tears poured down Pedro's cheeks. He thought the world of his dogs. He knew every hair on their backs, every wag of their tails.

"Didn't I tell you it would be best not to trust him!" yelled Ravelini, almost beside himself with rage and distress. "Well, the show will have to start, and we must put in another turn instead of the dogs. The goats will have to perform twice. We must send for the police and get them to look for the dogs for us."

What a to-do there was in the camp then! Soon everyone knew what had happened. The police were sent for, and soon two of them were busy taking down descriptions of each of the dogs. They were worth a great deal of money, and Mr. Ravelini could not afford to lose even one of them. Besides, he loved them just as Pedro did.

"Perhaps this will teach you not to hide rogues like Dick again," stormed Mr. Ravelini to poor Pedro, quite forgetting that he had said people must stand by their friends. "So you hid him in Leppi's kennel? I thought as much! Well, I must change into my ring suit. Get out of my way. I've no patience with you. If you hadn't disobeyed me over that new horse, you wouldn't have damaged your legs and could have looked after the dogs properly yourself. Tiresome pest of a boy!"

Poor Pedro! He had never in his life been so miserable—and he couldn't help feeling that his uncle was right. It *was* really his fault!

CHAPTER TWELVE

DICK FINDS LARRY AND THE DOGS

AND now, what was happening to Larry, Dick, and the dogs? Well, Larry had gone at a very good pace, all the dogs following excitedly at his heels. Into the heathery hills he went, and then sent the dogs in all directions by shouting, "Rabbits! Get them then! Rabbits!"

There really were rabbits, too—just coming out for their evening meal. So the dogs had the time of their lives, rushing after the bobtailed rabbits, and trying to dig them out of their burrows.

Larry lay down for a few minutes' rest. He was out of sight of the camp, and was delighted to know that his plan had been such a success. Aha! What would old Ravelini say when he found that his dogs were all gone?

Then Larry heard footsteps—and round a gorse

bush came Dick, his cheeks red, his breath coming fast, for he had run like a hare up the hills. Larry leapt to his feet and faced him. He glared at Dick in astonishment and rage.

"What do you want?" he shouted.

"The dogs!" panted Dick. "You scoundrel, Larry! I know what you meant to do to Pedro—lose his dogs for him, and blame me for it! I was hiding in the kennel and I heard all you said."

"Oh, you did, did you?" said Larry, his face red with anger. "Well, I've had enough of you and your interfering ways. Take that!"

Larry sprang at Dick, and hit him straight in the face. It was a heavy blow, and poor Dick staggered back, his lip bleeding. Larry came at him again, and Dick put up his fists, knowing that he had a very poor chance against Larry, who was bigger than he was, and much stronger.

But Dick was not a coward. He was not going to run away, even if he was beaten. Larry hit him again, this time on the side of the head, and Dick fell to the ground.

But someone else came into the fight now—someone with sharp white teeth and a fearsome growl—good old Bouncer. He was not going to see his master hit like that! What was a dog for if not to protect the person he loved?

So Bouncer joined in the fight. He had no fists to hit with—but he had a mouth to bite with! In a trice he had Larry pinned by the ankle, and the boy did not dare to move. He was terrified.

"Call your dog off!" he shouted. "He's got me by the ankle. Call him off or I'll kick him."

Dick sat up and rubbed his ear. He looked at Larry standing there, with Bouncer at his ankle, and he grinned.

"*I* shan't call him off!" he said. "It serves you right. Don't you move an inch, or Bouncer will bury his teeth into your leg. As long as you keep still you'll be all right. My, I could give you a good punch now, if I liked, couldn't I?"

But Dick didn't punch Larry, for Larry could not defend himself now. Besides, he must get the dogs as soon as he could. He stood and looked round. Leppi was still by him, growling hard. But the others were nowhere to be seen.

Dick whistled. He shouted their names. He whistled again. Not a dog came. Dick turned to Larry.

"Whistle the dogs," he commanded. "Go on—I've heard you do it before, and they'll come for your whistle."

Larry would not whistle. He stood there, his face sulky. Not a thing would he do to get the dogs back for Dick. Dick spoke to Bouncer.

"Worry him, then, Bouncer, worry him!"

Bouncer growled happily and closed his teeth a little more tightly on Larry's trousered leg. Larry gave a yell.

"I'll whistle! I'll whistle!" he cried. And he whistled loudly and long.

From far and near came the seven dogs, scampering up obediently. They ran round the two boys, their tails wagging and their tongues hanging out. Only Bouncer kept still, worrying at Larry's trouser leg. He was not really hurting the boy, but Larry knew that he would love to dig his teeth into him if only Dick said the word.

"Good dogs, good dogs!" said Dick to the fox terriers. "Home then—come along! Bouncer, stay where you are, and guard Larry. Guard him, then, guard him!"

"Gr-rr-rr-rr!" said Bouncer happily. Dick left Larry and Bouncer, knowing quite well that his dog would not let the boy escape. Down the hill he tore with the dogs, wondering if he would be in time for the show.

And the first thing he saw when he came in sight of the circus was—a pair of policemen! Dick did not know that they had come about the stolen dogs. He thought they had come to look for him again, and his heart sank into his boots. Now what was he to do?

He stood and thought. Then he made up his mind. He must take the dogs back to poor old Pedro, even though it meant being caught. Pedro had been so decent to him—now he must be good to Pedro, too. So down the last slope ran Dick, all the eight dogs at his heels. He squeezed through the hedge and ran into the field.

Philippo saw him first and gave a great shout: "There are the dogs!"

Everyone turned to look. As soon as Ravelini saw Dick, he called to the policemen nearby. "That's the boy! Catch him!"

Dick found himself between two big policemen. He called to Mr. Ravelini.

"Mr. Ravelini, sir! I didn't take the dogs! Larry did. I saw him!"

Pedro came limping over to the crowd round Dick, and caressed his dogs in joy. At first, so pleased was he to have his dogs back again, that he took no notice of Dick—and then he heard what he was saying.

"Larry took them?" he cried. "How do you know? Mrs. Dooly said you went off with them—she said you had Leppi and Bouncer, because she saw them!"

"Oh, do listen to me!" begged Dick, and he quickly told all his tale. "And if you don't believe me," he cried, "go up the hills, and you'll find my dog Bouncer guarding Larry. He'll tell you that I took the dogs from him."

"I think the boy is telling the truth," said Ravelini. "But why did you come back yourself, Dick, when you knew you might be caught?"

"I wanted to give Pedro back his dogs," said Dick. "He's been so decent to me, and I guessed he'd be miserable about his dogs. Are they in time for the show, sir?"

"Land's sakes! The show!" cried Mr. Ravelini. "The people are already at the gate! Quick! To your places, all of you. Pedro and Dick, manage the dogs!"

And to the enormous surprise of the two policemen, all the circus folk disappeared in a trice, running to the tent, and to the cages to get their animals. Dick took the dogs to their cage with Pedro, to brush them down and give them water.

"Seems as if we're not wanted here any more," said one of the policemen, shutting his notebook with a snap. "Pity we can't see the circus now we're here."

"I think it's our duty to," said the second policeman, with a grin. "There's been some funny business here today, and it's time we looked into it. Come into the big tent, and we'll find seats."

CHAPTER THIRTEEN

THE NEW CIRCUS BOY!

"DICK," said Pedro, as they got the dogs ready, "what about you getting into my circus suit, and seeing if you can help my uncle? I believe my suit would fit you all right. We're about the same size."

Pedro sat down on a bench in the dogs' cage to rest his legs. Dick looked at him in the greatest delight. "Go into the *ring*!" he said. "Oh, Pedro! Do you suppose Mr. Ravelini would let me?"

"We won't ask him!" said Pedro, with a grin. "I'll dress you up in my suit, and you can take the dogs into the ring when Ravelini cracks his whip for them. He will think that Yosif or Philippo will bring them in, and then go out—but *you* can go in! Do you remember all that Larry did in the ring with Uncle the other night?"

"I remember it perfectly," said Dick, his face burning with excitement. "Oh, quick, Pedro—let's go and see if your suit fits me!"

Dick helped Pedro to his caravan. It was empty. Pedro took a bright yellow suit out of a chest, and showed Dick the spangled cloak that went with it, and the jaunty, feathered cap. "There you are!" he said. "Isn't it grand?"

Dick stared at it. It certainly *was* grand! He stripped off his own old clothes, and tried on Pedro's circus suit. It was a bit tight in the waist, and the sleeves were a little long, but otherwise it fitted him perfectly. Pedro gave a whoop of delight.

"You look gorgeous! Look—is that Mrs. Dooly outside? Let's call her in to alter the waist a bit. You look as if you're going to burst out of my coat there!"

Mrs. Dooly came in, and stared in surprise at Dick. She soon let out the waist a bit for him, and turned in the sleeves. Then Dick brushed his hair well, and slipped out to get the dogs.

"Wish I could see you in the ring, Dick, old chap!" shouted Pedro. "Good luck!"

Pedro was back in his bunk. His legs were rapidly getting better, but they got tired very easily. He lay and wondered how Dick was getting on.

Dick was waiting behind the great curtains with eight dogs. He was trembling with excitement. Mr. Ravelini was in the ring, cracking his whip to his beautful horses as they danced in time to the music.

Then Mr. Roony went in with his elephants, and soon Dick heard shouts of laughter as they batted the ball, and sent it flying across the ring. Then in went Yosif, Philippo and Bella, and performed their marvellous and graceful tricks high on the trapeze in the roof.

And now it was the dogs' turn. As soon as the acrobats came out off the ring, followed by tremendous clapping, Mr. Ravelini cracked his whip for the next turn—his eight clever dogs! Their tails wagged. They gave little yelps of excitement. They knew it was their turn!

"Come along then!" said Dick. And into the ring he went, surrounded by the eight happy dogs. He bowed this way and that, just as he had seen Larry do, and the people clapped. Ravelini took one look at him and saw that it was Dick.

He cracked his whip twice. The dogs took their places, each on his own special stool. Dick looked pleadingly at the ringmaster. Was he going to be allowed to stay in the ring, or would he be sent out?

"You can stay," said Ravelini—"but don't get in my way!"

So Dick stayed. All the dogs could walk easily on their hind legs, and some of them could turn head-over heels in a clever and comical way. After each trick they were supposed to go back to their own stools, and some of them didn't want to. Dick quietly patted the right stools for the excited dogs, and got them back there every time, ready for the next trick.

The turn went very well indeed. The dogs liked Dick, and obeyed him when he called them after the

The dogs liked Dick and obeyed him

tricks. He quietened them, and Mr. Ravelini found that his dogs performed excellently that evening. He was pleased. He bowed at the end of his performance, and so did Dick. Storms of clapping and cheering greeted them.

The ringmaster bowed again, whistled to his dogs, and, putting his arm on Dick's shoulder, marched out of the ring. Dick was so proud! To think that the ringmaster had put his arm on his shoulder, and shown everyone that he, Dick, was part of the show! The boy looked up at Ravelini and thought he was the grandest man in the world.

"Dogs did well tonight, sir," called out Mr. Roony.

"They did," said Ravelini, "and I know why! They like this boy. He knows how to manage those dogs of mine. They never liked Larry in the ring with them."

Dick went to put the dogs away, his heart jumping with joy. Then he gave them a good meal, saw that their straw was fresh, and tore off to tell Pedro what had happened. Pedro listened in delight. He gave Dick a friendly punch and kicked his legs in the air.

"Good for you!" he said. "Good for you! Get out of my suit now, in case you dirty it."

As Dick was taking it off, a thought flashed into his mind. Bouncer. He'd forgotten about Bouncer for the last two hours—and, good gracious, Larry was still up on the hill, with Bouncer holding him by the leg!

"Well," said Dick, "fancy me forgetting that, Pedro! Larry's still up on the hills with Bouncer. Had you forgotten him, too?"

"Oh no," said Pedro, grinning. "I was thinking it was a fine punishment for Larry! He won't like being stuck up there at all. But will you have to go and get him, Dick? Blow."

"I'd better," said Dick, putting on his own clothes. "He's a tiresome scamp, but I can't leave him all night long, though I'd love to. Anyway, I want Bouncer. I'll go and get them both."

"He'll get into fine trouble with uncle," said Pedro. "I bet he'll get a beating this time!"

Dick ran off up the hills—but he hadn't got far before he saw Larry and Bouncer! Bouncer had got tired of guarding Larry so far away from the camp, and had had the bright idea of taking him back there. He had loosed his teeth from Larry's trousers, and had made him go down the path towards the camp, just as if Larry were a sheep to be taken back to the fold!"

"Larry! Bouncer!" cried Dick in astonishment. "My word, Larry, you're going to get into trouble now—and serve you right."

"Let me go, please, Dick," said Larry in a humble voice. "I'm afraid to go back to the camp. Ravelini will send me back to my father and he is cruel to me. You know how you hated to think you might go back to the Home—well, give *me* a chance, won't you? I know I've been beastly to you and Pedro, and I wish I hadn't now. Give me a chance, Dick, and let me go. I can find a job somewhere else."

Dick never bore anyone malice. He whistled to Bouncer, who came gladly to his heels. "All right," he said to Larry. "You can run off. I won't stop you.

I've no wish to see you beaten, though I think you deserve it. Goodbye—and good luck!"

Larry was not used to hearing anyone wish him good luck. He stared at Dick, and for the first time he wished that he was more like the sort of boy that Dick was. He put out his hand in a shamefaced way. "Goodbye and good luck to you, too," he said.

Dick shook hands. Then he and Bouncer went back to the camp, and Larry fled away in the darkening night, making up his mind for the first time in his life to try and be decent.

As Dick came into the camp he saw Mr. Ravelini talking to the two policemen, who had watched the show. Ravelini called to Dick. "Come here! I was talking about you, my boy!"

Dick went up. Ravelini clapped him on the back and beamed at him. "I've just been asking these policemen to tell Mr. Harris that I've got a job for you in my circus," he said. "These men saw you perform tonight, and they agree with me that you can do well. There's no need for you to go back to the Home if you can get a job and keep it!"

"Oh, thanks, Mr. Ravelini," said Dick, hardly believing the good news. "It's jolly good of you. I'll do my best in every way—and I'm so glad to know I can stay with old Pedro."

Dick rushed off to tell Pedro, who shouted and whooped for joy so loudly that Mr. Ravelini came to see what was the matter, and Bouncer really looked quite scared.

"Uncle, you're a real good sport!" yelled Pedro. "Dick's my friend, and always will be! He can go into the ring until I'm well—and then we'll work up